Badlands

Anna Kenna

illustrated by Warren Mahy

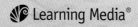
Learning Media®

Contents

1. Beans

Krystal tucked the can of beans into her pocket and crept along the subway tracks. She carefully balanced her feet, focusing on the car in front of her. A distant cough reminded her she needed to be quick. Nervously, she looked back to the car where the others slept. She hoped nobody would miss her.

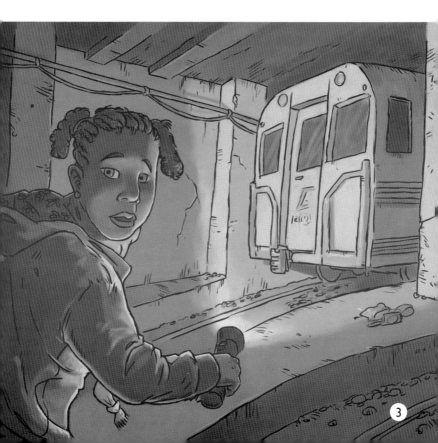

Apart from her tattered clothes, there wasn't much to remind Krystal of her life before the meteor had struck. Along with the other survivors, the subway station had become her home – if that were the right word for it.

Krystal reached the car that was tucked away where the track branched off. She climbed inside and shined her flashlight around. A pale boy covered his eyes and scampered to his feet. "It's OK, Paul," said Krystal. "It's only me. I've brought you some food."

Instead of answering, Paul started coughing. His face turned red, and his eyes streamed. Krystal frowned. "You're spending too much time up in the Badlands," she said. Paul still didn't reply. He looked hungrily at the can.

After he'd eaten, Paul went to sleep. Krystal quietly closed the car door, switched off her flashlight, and tiptoed back to her own car. Thankfully, everybody was still asleep – everybody except Brogan.

2. Trust

Krystal was shaken awake. She'd been dreaming. Like all her dreams over the last few months, it had been a bad one. She sat up, her heart sinking. She knew what this would be about.

Troy was standing over her, and Brogan stood behind him looking smug. "You've been giving our food to Paul, haven't you?" Troy said. Krystal didn't answer.

"Haven't you?" repeated Troy.

"He's sick," said Krystal.

"Well, we're sick of him," said Troy.

"Paul was a part of our community, and he blew it," said Brogan sourly.

Krystal looked away. She knew Paul had asked for everything he got ... making secret trips to the Badlands ... not sharing what he'd found. Still, she couldn't stand by and watch him starve.

"What did you give him?" asked Troy.

"Beans. She gave him a can of beans," said Brogan. "She used a flashlight, too."

"Did you?" asked Troy. His eyes were blazing.

"Yes," replied Krystal in a tiny voice.

An hour later, with her few possessions in her backpack, Krystal stood looking down the tracks. It was impossible to see without a flashlight, but Krystal knew what lay ahead: long, dark tunnels that led nowhere. And now she was alone.

Krystal's friends had pleaded with Troy to give her a second chance, but he wouldn't. "We can't trust her. She has to go," he'd said.

Maybe if Brogan hadn't been there, Krystal would have stood a chance. She could have explained. But Brogan had always been jealous of Krystal – she didn't know why. Brogan had watched Krystal collect her things. She had smiled the whole time, sometimes whispering to Troy. No doubt Brogan was making him feel better about what he'd done.

For the second time that night, with Troy's words ringing in her ears, Krystal began to walk.

3. Outcast

Krystal was dreaming it was her birthday. She was tearing open a big present – but something was wrong. The tearing sound was too real. She woke with a jolt. Rats! They were swarming all over her backpack.

"Get out!" Krystal yelled. The hungry creatures continued to tear at her bag. She kicked at them, but it was no use.

"Scram!" A figure charged out of the
darkness and pointed something at the rats.
Whoosh! White foam spewed from a fire
extinguisher. The startled creatures ran up
the walls and disappeared.

"There's not much food left," said Paul, shining a weak light on the remains of Krystal's backpack.

"There wasn't much to start with," said Krystal. "They only gave me some crackers and a jar of peanut butter."

"They're the real rats," said Paul bitterly.
He started coughing again. It was a dry,
hacking cough that he'd had for weeks.
It had taken a long time to find some cough
medicine, and it hadn't made any difference.
Paul needed sunshine and fresh air.

"So, what do we do now?" Krystal asked.

"These could be a start," Paul croaked.
He opened his hand. In the gloom, Krystal
could just make out a bunch of keys.

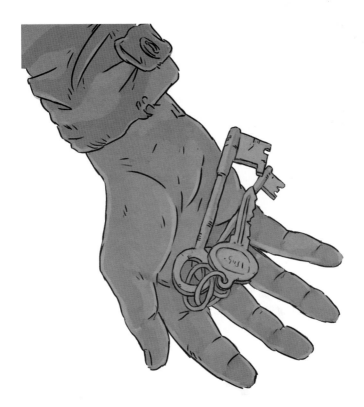

4. Ambush

Krystal and Paul came out of the subway. Gray skies, freezing cold, and choking smoke greeted them. The sun hadn't shone for months, and there was no sign of life. The sight still shocked Krystal, even though she'd been up to the Badlands many times.

Krystal pulled her scarf up over her nose and squinted in the dim light. Paul pulled the hood of his jacket over his face. The fumes always sent him into fits of coughing.

Carefully, they began to pick their way through the rubble. There were no longer any streets or sidewalks. Everything was a jumble of broken concrete and twisted metal.

Krystal had been furious when she'd learned about the keys. Paul had found them in a police station on his first trip to the Badlands. "There was a tag. I think they're for some kind of storeroom," he'd said. "There might be food there."

"You had no right to keep them for yourself," Krystal had yelled.

Paul had just shrugged. "I was waiting till I'd found the storeroom. So, are you going to help me look?"

They passed a supermarket that had been stripped bare, then the remains of a shopping mall. Hundreds of burned-out cars were parked nearby.

Suddenly, Paul stopped.

"What is it?" Krystal's voice was muffled by her scarf.

"There's somebody here," whispered Paul. They saw something move behind one of the cars. It was difficult to tell what – or who – it was. Then Brogan stepped into the gray light.

"Well, well," she sneered. "I wonder what you two are doing?" Before Krystal could reply, somebody grabbed her from behind and pushed her to the ground. Rough hands searched her clothing. She could see the same thing happening to Paul.

"Get off me!" Paul cried angrily. Even though he was weak, he twisted around, trying to shake off Brogan's friends.

"Got them!" said a male voice. Krystal heard the keys jangle.

"You should be more careful about what you discuss in the dark," called Brogan as the group hurried away.

5. Thief

After the keys had been taken, Paul seemed to give up. He lay on his dirty mattress, coughing again and again. Krystal sat beside him. She could hear people chatting down the tracks. She missed the others. Maybe one day, they'd take her back. While Paul slept, she plotted. Later, she slipped away.

Krystal crouched in the shadows until she was certain it was safe, then she sneaked into the car. She knelt beside the sleeping Brogan. Searching through her backpack, she found a cellphone, an address book, a pair of worn shoes, and some coins – but no keys. Brogan stirred and rolled onto her back. Krystal was just about to search Brogan's pockets when a hand grabbed her shoulder.

"Our thief strikes again," said Troy, peering down at her.

"Brogan's the thief!" yelled Krystal, her eyes brimming with tears. "The keys are mine." Krystal's loud voice woke Brogan. Troy listened as Krystal told him about how she and Paul had been ambushed. When she'd finished, Troy turned to Brogan.

"Give Krystal her keys," he commanded. Brogan shrugged and tried to look innocent. "Give them back!" Troy repeated in a low voice. He looked angry – and tired.

Slowly, Brogan reached into her jacket pocket and fumbled around. Troy snatched the keys from her hand. "Have you learned nothing, Brogan? If everyone's a thief, no one will survive."

Troy handed the keys to Krystal. She expected him to ask what they were for, but he didn't. "You have what you came for. Now go." Their eyes met. Krystal opened her mouth to speak, even though she didn't know what she wanted to say. But Troy wasn't giving her a second chance.

"Go," he repeated.

6. Secrets

The keys lay in Krystal's hand. She ran her fingers along their jagged edges. She wished they could tell her where to go. Her thumb felt something rough on the flat side of the biggest key. Krystal clicked on Paul's flashlight. She could just make out the engraved letters C.H.H.Q. She flicked off the flashlight, whispering to herself. She frowned. H.Q. had to stand for headquarters – but C.H.? Crisis? City?

"City Hall!" Krystal said out loud. "Yes!" she whispered. She woke Paul.

In the freezing wind, they picked their way toward City Hall. Paul's cough was worse than ever, and he had to keep stopping to rest. Finally, they stood looking at the once grand building. The pillars at the entrance had collapsed, and the roof had caved in.

They walked around the side of the building and found a door. It took all of their strength to force it open, then they followed two flights of stairs to a basement parking garage. Cars waited in neat rows for drivers who would never return. Krystal tried to remember the last time she'd ridden in a car, but she couldn't. Cars belonged to another lifetime.

On the far side of the parking garage, they found another door and followed a corridor that ran deep into the building. At the end of the corridor, a third staircase stopped at a metal door. The sign on the door read C.H.H.Q.

With her heart pounding, Krystal slid the key into the lock and turned it. The door swung open.

Inside, a large room was stacked with bedding, canned food, bottled water, and medical supplies. Paul wandered around in a daze. Krystal leaned against the door. "We've found it," she whispered. "We've found it."

"It's all ours," said Paul, his eyes darting about. "Our secret."

Krystal looked at her friend. He was so thin, and his skin was the color of milk. She pulled a soft gray blanket over his shoulders.

"Don't you think secrets have cost us enough?" she asked.

DIGGING DEEPER

Meteors and Meteorites

The word meteor comes from the Greek word meteoron, which means "a thing in the sky." A meteor is a piece of space rock from a comet or a piece of space junk that has entered Earth's atmosphere. Meteors can be as small as a grain of sand or as big as a shopping mall. As they speed through Earth's atmosphere, they heat up and glow. This is what we call a shooting star.

Once they're in Earth's atmosphere, most meteors break up or burn out before they hit the ground. A meteor that manages to survive this journey falls into the ocean or onto land. This is called a meteorite.

Scientists believe that this large crater in Arizona was created by a meteorite around fifty thousand years ago. The crater is over 4,000 feet (1.2 kilometers) wide and 570 feet (152 meters) deep.

Meteorite Strike

Every day, up to four billion meteorites hit Earth, but most of them are too small to cause any damage. Scientists believe that a meteorite big enough to create a global disaster, such as the one in the story, is likely to hit Earth only once or twice every million years. Nobody knows exactly what effect this would have, but scientists have made some predictions.

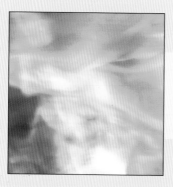

1. The heat created by the impact would turn rock into gas and start huge fires.

2. These gases would poison the air, and the fires would create huge clouds of smoke and soot.

3. There would be tidal waves and flooding near the coast.

4. The dust, smoke, and poisons in the air would keep the sun's light and heat from reaching Earth. Plants would die from lack of sunlight, and animals would die of starvation or freeze to death.

5. It would take several years for the atmosphere to clear. Only then would plants begin to grow, giving the survivors fresh food to eat.

WEIGHING BOTH SIDES

All for One and One for All

There is never a good time for a disaster to strike. Earthquakes, volcanic eruptions, and floods can cause loss of life and huge damage. It can sometimes take months, or even years, for a community to get back on its feet. Repairs to buildings, roads, and other services take time.

However, disasters can often bring out the good things in people. After a disaster, people usually look after each other and share resources such as food, clothing, and shelter. They also help to rescue others from danger and treat their injuries. The subway community in this story helped each other by sharing possessions and agreeing to rules that would benefit everybody.

By studying the effects of a disaster, experts can help us to prepare for similar disasters in the future.